9/11 A Survivor's Story

I0811681

Lorin Driggs

Consultant

Jennifer M. Lopez, NBCT, M.S.Ed.
Teacher Specialist—History/Social Studies
Office of Curriculum & Instruction
Norfolk Public Schools

Publishing Credits

Rachelle Cracchiolo, M.S.Ed., *Publisher*
Conni Medina, M.A.Ed., *Editor in Chief*
Emily R. Smith, M.A.Ed., *Content Director*
Véronique Bos, *Creative Director*
Robin Erickson, *Art Director*
Michelle Jovin, M.A., *Associate Editor*
Lee Aucoin, *Senior Graphic Designer*

Image Credits: front cover, p.1 AP Photo/Amy Sancetta; back cover, p.19, p.20, p.21 (top and bottom) courtesy Lorin Driggs; p.6 AP Photo/Carmen Taylor; p.7 David Handschuh/NY Daily News Archive via Getty Images; p.8 Doug Kanter/AFP/Getty Images; p.9 Photo by Eric Draper, courtesy of the George W. Bush Presidential Library; p.10 NYPD; p.11 AP Photo/Pool, Keith Meyers/The New York Times; p.12 Corey Sipkin/NY Daily News Archive via Getty Images; p.13 Spencer Platt/Getty Images; p.14 Lawrence Schwartzwald/Splashnews/Newscom; p.15 Tannen Maury/AFP/Getty Images; p.16 Reuters/Newscom; p.17 AP Photo/Navy Times, Mark Faram; p.18, p.20 Marla Mayer/Fotogloria/UIG via Getty Images; p.19 Mario Tama/Getty Images; p.22 Jose Jimenez/Primera Hora/Getty Images; p.23 Shutterworx/iStock; p.24 Anthony Correia/Shutterstock; p.25 Porter Gifford/Corbis via Getty Images; p.25 Peter Ginter/Science Faction/Getty Images; p.26 Roberto Schmidt/AFP/Getty Images; p.29 (top) Gagliardi Photography/Shutterstock; p.31 Steve Heap/Shutterstock; p.32 2001 The Record (Bergen Co. NJ)/Getty Images; all other images from iStock and/or Shutterstock.

This book may not be reproduced or distributed in any way without prior consent from the publisher. All companies, websites, and products mentioned in this book are registered trademarks of their respective owners or developers and are used in this book strictly for editorial purposes. No commercial claim to their use is made by the author or the publisher.

TCM Teacher Created Materials
5301 Oceanus Drive
Huntington Beach, CA 92649-1030
www.tcmpub.com
ISBN 978-1-6449-1012-2
© 2020 Teacher Created Materials, Inc.

Table of Contents

Day 1: It Begins

8:46 a.m., September 11, 2001

People remember what a beautiful morning it was in New York City. I was getting ready to leave for a business meeting. I stopped to open the bedroom windows to let the clean, crisp air in. Suddenly, there was a very loud, thudding crash from somewhere outside. Lilly came rushing out from the other side of the apartment, and we met in the living room.

"What was that?" we said in unison. We looked out the window, which faced south. People on the sidewalks and street below were running. Some people were heading west, toward the park that stretches along the Hudson River behind our apartment complex. Other people were running toward the World Trade Center, a block and a half to the east, out of view from our apartment.

The morning news on TV was interrupted with a report that a plane had crashed into 1 World Trade Center, the northernmost of the Twin Towers. It was unclear whether it was a small private plane or passenger jet. However, there could be no doubt about one thing: an accident like this would be devastating for the people in the plane and in the building.

Accident. That's what everyone thought at first, but soon we would learn the terrible, terrifying truth.

Battery Park City

Lilly and I lived in the Gateway Plaza apartment complex in Battery Park City. Battery Park City is a residential neighborhood built on the west side of Lower Manhattan. When Battery Park City was first built, workers used dirt and debris from the **excavation** that took place for the construction of the World Trade Center's Twin Towers.

The sunrise casts an orange glow on the Twin Towers.

9:03 a.m.

It wasn't long before the plane was identified as a large commercial passenger jet. On TV, a camera showed the burning North Tower in the **foreground** and the **picturesque** blue sky beyond. Looking closely at the TV, I noticed a dark speck in the air in the distance over New Jersey and realized I could see that same view from our living room window. I looked out and saw the speck growing larger and larger as it approached the Hudson River from the west. It was a big jet, flying directly toward us. The roar of the jet's engines was **deafening** as it flew past our building. In a split second, there was another thudding, shattering crash, even louder than the one from the first impact. The South Tower, 2 World Trade Center, had been hit. Now, we knew this was an attack, not an accident.

I took the elevator down and hurried out into the garden in the center of our apartment complex. Looking up at the two World Trade Center towers, what I saw was almost impossible for me to understand. Flames and smoke were **billowing** out of both buildings. Other residents were gathering in the garden to stare at the shocking sight, and Lilly appeared at my side. "It's not safe here," she said. "Come back inside."

A passenger jet strikes the South Tower.

Live on Television

After the first plane struck the North Tower, people around the world rushed to their television sets. They wanted answers and turned to news stations for the latest information. As people dealt with their shock, they saw a small speck appear on their TV screens. Then, millions of people around the world were forced to watch helplessly as the second plane crashed into the South Tower.

NO STANDING
NO STANDING
EXCEPT TRUCKS
ONE WAY
ANN TAYLOR

9:59 a.m.

We were still watching the news coverage on TV when there was a deep rumbling—a rumbling we could both hear and feel. The windows across the street turned deep red, reflecting fire. Then, as if someone flicked off a light switch, all light disappeared from our world. Something as dark as midnight was blocking the sun, and the power went out.

Slowly, dim daylight began to emerge. Panicked, I grabbed my wallet and cell phone, and Lilly grabbed our apartment keys. We locked the door and rushed down six floors of stairs to the lobby.

Outside, the air was swirling with thick, gray dust that fell like textured rain. It covered the trees, bushes, sidewalks, and grass. It clung to the hair, skin, and clothes of people. It transformed us into ghostly shapes against a **monotone** gray background. Everyone was stunned and terrified even before we learned the unimaginable truth: the South Tower, the one closest to us, had collapsed.

More frightened and confused residents gathered in the lobby. Then, seemingly out of nowhere, emergency workers in bright orange vests appeared. They told us we had to leave the area immediately. They directed us toward the Battery Park City **Esplanade**, which runs along the Hudson River.

◀ Survivors fled through swirling gray dust.

The President Speaks

At the time of the World Trade Center attacks, President George W. Bush was in Sarasota, Florida. He was reading to children in a classroom at Emma E. Booker Elementary School. His first address to the nation about the attacks was made from the school, with students standing behind him.

The South Tower Collapses

Each Twin Tower had 110 floors. When the South Tower collapsed, it was leveled in about 10 seconds.

10:28 a.m.

The crowd of residents and workers from nearby office buildings headed south on the esplanade in a grim, determined march. Suddenly, there was another deafening roar. We looked back and saw a cloud of dust, ash, and debris rolling toward us. Some people screamed and started to run, but to no **avail**. In seconds, we were completely surrounded by a wind of blinding white dust and smoke. The North Tower had collapsed.

Next to me, a **plaintive** voice rose above the chaos: "I'm alone." It was an elderly woman, moving with difficulty in the rushing crowd. I reached out and took her hand. Lilly, who was up ahead, called to me, "Come on!"

"I'm coming," I shouted. "I'll catch up!" Arm-in-arm, the woman and I continued toward whatever lie ahead.

Near the end of the esplanade, boats of all kinds—fishing boats, tugboats, ferries, police boats, and fireboats—appeared in the Hudson River to take people off the island. Lilly and I helped the elderly woman into one boat, then waited for our turn, eventually climbing into a New York City police boat. As it chugged out into the river toward New Jersey, I looked back at Lower Manhattan. Dust and smoke smothered the buildings like a **shroud**, and the two towers of the World Trade Center were gone.

Boats raced between New York and New Jersey to rescue survivors. ▶

Historic Boatlift

Before 9/11, the largest evacuation by boat in history occurred in Dunkirk, France, during World War II. In that evacuation, 338,000 **Allied troops** were evacuated across the English Channel over the course of nine days. That evacuation rate was about 1,500 people per hour. On September 11, nearly 500,000 people were evacuated by boat from Lower Manhattan in nine hours. That evacuation rate is more than 55,000 people per hour.

Evacuation across the River

The police boat took us to a pier on the New Jersey side of the river. We were directed toward a wide expanse of paved walkways in front of several tall modern office buildings. I don't know how many of us there were, but there were a lot, with more arriving all the time. No one could tell us what we were supposed to do next. Workers from the office buildings brought out chairs, water, and even food for the **evacuees**. They escorted us into the buildings to use their companies' bathrooms. There was so much kindness and anxiety and so little information.

I had my cell phone, so Lilly and I were able to call our families to tell them we were okay. That's how we learned what people across the country and around the world were seeing on TV—survivors covered head to toe in gray dust emerging like ghosts from the area around the World Trade Center. Firefighters and police officers rushing in. Nearby buildings damaged. Cars crushed. Smoke. Chaos. Terror.

We spent the day there, sitting outside in the beautiful weather, watching a nightmare unfolding on the other side of the Hudson River.

A police officer helps a survivor after the North Tower collapsed.

A Niece's Perspective

My niece Lorin was 16 years old when the World Trade Center was attacked. She wrote to me two days afterward: "I'm so overwhelmed with happiness that both of you are safe and secure.... My school did not allow us to watch the events unfold on TV, so I was unsure of the real damage until I arrived home. I don't think I've ever been so upset/sad/scared/angry in my entire life. So many people died...so many families ruined.... When I first heard, I was in shock. It was like a movie.... About an hour later, it had all sunk in and hit me like a ton of bricks. I felt panicked and worried and couldn't control my emotions.... Mom explained that she had talked with you and that you were alive and well."

Survivors walk through the streets of Lower Manhattan as dust from the collapse of the Twin Towers swirls around them.

Lilly and I didn't know what we could do or should do. Where would we spend the night? And what about tomorrow? When could we go home, and would our home even be there?

Word spread among the evacuees that a temporary Red Cross shelter had been set up farther up the river, and we set out to find it. We found the shelter on the first floor of an unfinished building with a wall of windows giving a perfect view across the river.

Food was brought in—hamburgers and fries from a fast-food restaurant. Cots were set up in rows. Red Cross workers took everyone's names and handed out toothbrushes and socks. People from the neighborhood arrived and offered their extra rooms to strangers. Emergency medical technicians tended to those who were most **distressed**. Everyone was kind, considerate, and concerned.

Smoke filled the New York City skyline in the early hours of September 12.

Unable to sleep, I looked around the vast, darkened room. Some people had brought their dogs, which now slept on the floor next to their owners' cots. Occasionally, someone coughed or a child cried. Several other restless, worried non-sleepers like me were **silhouetted** against the wall of windows that faced the river and the fire-glow of Lower Manhattan on the other side. It was a long night.

The Red Cross

The American Red Cross was founded in 1881. Its goal was to give help to people in need, especially soldiers and their families. Its workers also help victims of natural disasters, such as tornadoes, earthquakes, and fires. The Red Cross helps at large-scale accidents and terrorist attacks too. The Red Cross provides emergency shelter, food, and first aid and has a nationwide program for blood donations.

Day 2: Safe with Friends

The next morning, I was able to call our friends Sam and Carol just before my cell phone battery died. They lived in New Jersey, not far from the Red Cross shelter. Even in New Jersey, police and the **National Guard** blocked streets near the river, but eventually Sam was able to get close enough with his car so that we could walk to meet him. It's difficult to describe the emotions we felt when we saw him. On this particular day, our friend took on the appearance of our rescuer.

▼ A rescue helicopter flies by the still-burning Pentagon.

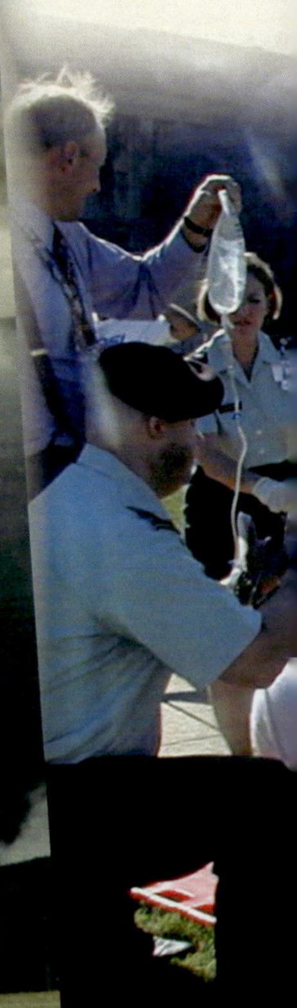

Lilly and I were still covered with thick gray dust. Even after a shower and a warm meal, we could not sleep, exhausted though we were. Instead, we watched TV nonstop, learning more about what had happened to us and to so many others. We were horrified to hear that another attack happened at the **Pentagon** in Arlington, Virginia, outside Washington, DC. There was also a hijacked plane that had crashed in a Pennsylvania field. Everywhere we turned, there was fear and destruction. We wondered who did this and why? What did it mean for us, for our city, and our country?

We had escaped and were safe. Now, we knew that thousands of others had not been so fortunate.

The Terrible Toll of 9/11

New York City, New York:
2,753 people were killed when two hijacked passenger planes were flown into the World Trade Center and the towers collapsed.

Arlington, Virginia:
184 people were killed when a hijacked passenger plane crashed into the Pentagon.

Near Shanksville, Pennsylvania:
40 people were killed when a hijacked passenger plane crashed into a field.

People aid a wounded man outside the Pentagon.

Day 3: A Difficult Trek to a Crime Scene

All transportation into and out of Manhattan was completely shut down until Thursday, September 13. On that day, Lilly and I decided to try to get back to our apartment. We had no idea if we could even get close. We wrote "Resident Gateway Plaza" in big black letters on T-shirts to identify ourselves as people who belonged there. Sam took us to the **ferry terminal** on the New Jersey side of the Hudson River.

We got off the ferry in Midtown Manhattan and boarded a city bus, hoping to get as close to Lower Manhattan as possible. The bus had traveled only a few blocks when the driver announced that the bus was being stopped and everyone had to get off. There had been a bomb scare nearby, and the streets were closed to traffic.

Lorin and Lilly's journey to their apartment ▶

We got out and started to walk. Our apartment was 60 blocks away; that's about three miles (five kilometers). At 14th Street, we encountered the first police **blockade**. We explained where we lived and were allowed to pass. The air became increasingly smoky and dusty the farther south we got. We stopped in a store and bought masks, hoping to protect our lungs from whatever was in the air.

▲ A police blockade stops people from entering the area around Lower Manhattan.

Coming Up to a Different World

More than half the people who live in New York City use public transportation. Less than two hours after the initial plane crash, the entire subway system had been shut down. People were evacuated from underground. Those who were evacuated near Lower Manhattan came to the surface and saw a completely changed world. One resident, Robert Rios, took the subway to school that morning. When he and other subway passengers were evacuated, Rios did not know the reason. When he reached street level, the North Tower was already burning. "It was like war," Rios later said.

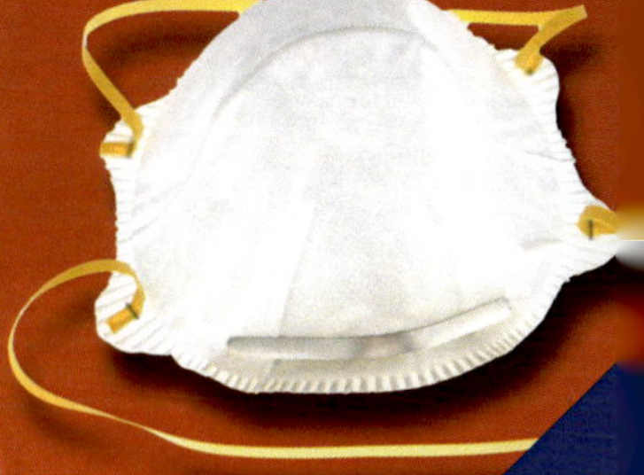

▼ Lorin and Lilly followed a member of the National Guard to their apartment.

Lilly and I finally made it to Battery Park at the southern tip of Manhattan. We found a group of people gathered there, including some of our neighbors. Eventually, we were allowed to go to our apartment. However, we had to be escorted by a member of the National Guard. Because of the ongoing search for clues and evidence, our apartment complex—the closest one to the Twin Towers—was still a **crime scene**.

A thick layer of gray dust and millions of sheets of paper—blown out of all those World Trade Center offices—covered everything. The electricity was still out. We walked up the six floors to our frighteningly dark, dust-coated apartment. We were allowed 10 minutes to gather what we needed. What we didn't know then was that we wouldn't live in our home again for nearly six weeks.

Now we faced the same long walk back to the ferry terminal. We got lucky, though, when someone told us that fishing boats were taking workers back and forth between Lower Manhattan and New Jersey. Workers were needed at the World Trade Center site, and there were thousands of volunteers. We walked over to the river, just south of where we had boarded the boat that carried us to safety days before. The fishing boat *Captain John* took us back to New Jersey.

▼ Lorin and Lilly crossed the Hudson River on the *Captain John*.

A Horrifying Reminder

We saw a chilling sight when we got on the fishing boat: hundreds of empty strollers and baby carriages. Parents and caretakers had left them when they climbed onto the boats to safety.

The National Guard

The New York Army National Guard was the foremost military organization in responding to the 9/11 attacks. Thousands of active and retired service members would help in the days and months after.

◀ Lorin and Lilly walked through their apartment's garden, where Lorin had stood on the morning of the attacks.

The Following Weeks: Closer to Home

Over the next few weeks, we moved a few times. We left Sam and Carol's home in New Jersey and went to a friend's Manhattan apartment. Finally, we got a room in a hotel. We returned to our jobs and worked toward returning home.

Someone set up a website where people in our neighborhood could post updates and share information. People posted about who was okay and who was still missing. There was information on how victims' families and **displaced** residents could get help. Long before Facebook® and Twitter™, this was an early example of social media in action.

Flyers appeared all over Lower Manhattan and around hospitals. On them were large photos of missing people. It was almost too sad to face.

The streets of Lower Manhattan remained closed except for official and emergency vehicles. We were able to get to our apartment from time to time with help from the National Guard and city officials. Sometimes, residents were loaded in the backs of pickup trucks and driven along the esplanade. Sometimes we walked in groups. We had to be escorted by police officers and members of the National Guard. Nothing was normal, and everything seemed hard. Yet, we kept looking ahead to when we could go home for good.

Restricted Access

Over one million workers and residents south of Canal Street had been evacuated in the hours following the attacks. Only emergency vehicles were allowed to enter Lower Manhattan. Vehicle traffic below Canal Street would not open back up until October 13.

▼ Emergency workers clear the wreckage of the World Trade Center in late September.

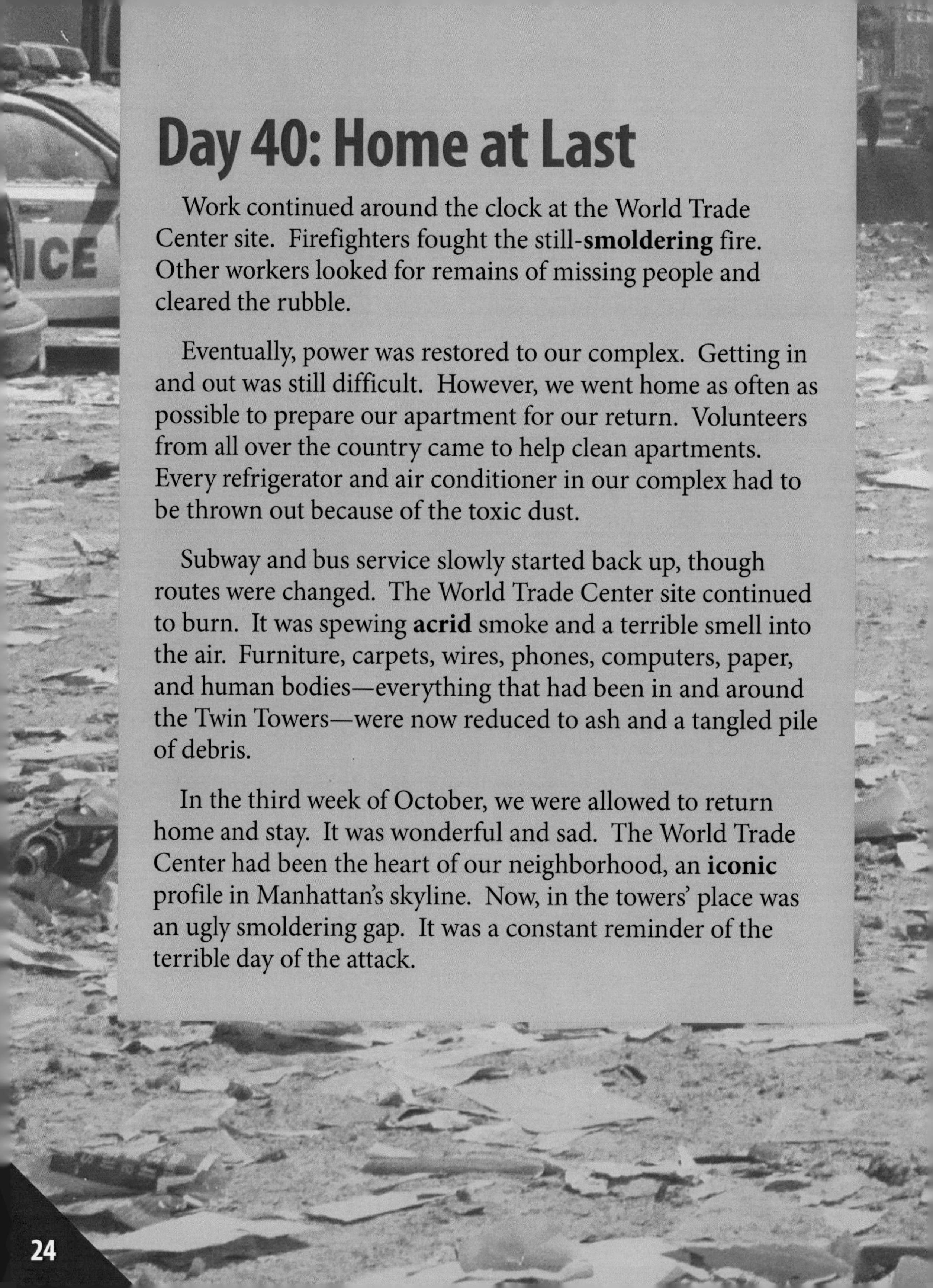

Day 40: Home at Last

Work continued around the clock at the World Trade Center site. Firefighters fought the still-**smoldering** fire. Other workers looked for remains of missing people and cleared the rubble.

Eventually, power was restored to our complex. Getting in and out was still difficult. However, we went home as often as possible to prepare our apartment for our return. Volunteers from all over the country came to help clean apartments. Every refrigerator and air conditioner in our complex had to be thrown out because of the toxic dust.

Subway and bus service slowly started back up, though routes were changed. The World Trade Center site continued to burn. It was spewing **acrid** smoke and a terrible smell into the air. Furniture, carpets, wires, phones, computers, paper, and human bodies—everything that had been in and around the Twin Towers—were now reduced to ash and a tangled pile of debris.

In the third week of October, we were allowed to return home and stay. It was wonderful and sad. The World Trade Center had been the heart of our neighborhood, an **iconic** profile in Manhattan's skyline. Now, in the towers' place was an ugly smoldering gap. It was a constant reminder of the terrible day of the attack.

▼ Workers cleaned dust from buildings around the World Trade Center.

The Long-Burning Fire

The fire at the World Trade Center site burned for months. It was finally extinguished on December 20, 2001—100 days after the attack.

Toxic Dust

Dust covered the area around the World Trade Center site. This dust contained more than 2,500 harmful substances. Today, more than 37,000 people have been diagnosed with at least one medical problem that came from the 9/11 attacks.

▼ The remains of the World Trade Center continued to smolder for months.

Epilogue

In the months that followed, we resumed our lives, but it was not easy. The World Trade Center site became a tourist attraction. Some people mourned and paid their respects. Other people posed in front of the gaping hole to have their pictures taken. Street vendors shouted out their offerings of T-shirts, photos, and other souvenirs. For many of us, this was a source of rage. How did people not recognize the area as the scene of a terrible tragedy? How did they not understand that thousands of people had died? How could they not think of the people who had experienced an unspeakable terror that day?

Today, the beautiful new One World Trade Center rises triumphantly in Lower Manhattan. The losses, terror, and heroism of that terrible day and the days, weeks, and months that followed are honored with an excellent memorial museum. Our old neighborhood has recovered. It is full of life once again.

Lilly and I live in another state now. We are fine, but sometimes, something reminds us of that day in 2001 and a bit of the fear rushes back. We never forget that our suffering was so small compared to those who lost people or those who barely escaped with their lives. That day and the days that followed brought us closer together. Through that tragedy, we learned so much about humanity, courage, perseverance, and our own strength.

Meeting Edith Again

9/11 support groups formed in our community, and Lilly joined one of those groups. At one meeting, an elderly woman named Edith told of being on the esplanade that day, calling out that she was alone, and being helped by two women. Lilly recognized the story. That was the beginning of a warm friendship that continues to this day.

▼ A city guide talks about the 9/11 attacks.

Memorialize It!

After the attacks on 9/11, a memorial museum was built at the site. The memorial site has many important design aspects. The new building is exactly 1,776 feet high. That number was chosen for the year the United States signed its independence. The observation deck at the building begins at 1,362 feet and extends to 1,368 feet. Those were the heights of the original Twin Towers. There are also two large square pools with waterfalls in the exact spots where the Twin Towers once stood. The pools contain the engraved names of all the victims from the attacks.

Each year, millions of people visit the museum to learn about and to remember that day. How would you want the 9/11 memorial to look? Reading this eyewitness account, what struck you as important about the original buildings? How would you want the feelings of the survivors to be expressed through your memorial? How would you honor the victims? Sketch out a plan for how your memorial would look with details about why you chose that design. Then, build your own memorial for that day.

One World Trade Center is now a memorial museum.

Glossary

acrid—unpleasantly sharp or irritating to the senses

Allied troops—members of the military of the nations united to fight the Axis powers during World War II

avail—use

billowing—moving and rising in the form of a large cloud

blockade—a barrier

crime scene—a place where a crime or serious offense occurred

deafening—extremely loud

displaced—refers to people who have been forced to leave the area where they live

distressed—showing or feeling extreme unhappiness or pain

esplanade—an open area of paved or grassy ground

evacuees—people who have been evacuated, or removed, from a dangerous place

excavation—the process of digging a hole in the ground by removing dirt and soil

ferry terminal—a place where boats, called *ferries*, can load people, cars, and goods for transportation

foreground—the part of a picture or scene that is nearest to the viewer

iconic—widely recognized; well-known

monotone—having one color

National Guard—the main standby military force that serves in the United States

Pentagon—the building that is the headquarters of the U.S. Department of Defense

picturesque—very charming or pretty

plaintive—seeming to be suffering or in need of help

shroud—a cover for the dead; used figuratively, something that covers from view

silhouetted—outlined

smoldering—burning slowly without flames but typically with smoke

Index

9/11 memorial in Pennsylvania

Your Turn!

This photograph was taken by photographer Thomas E. Franklin on September 11, 2001. It is titled *Raising the Flag at Ground Zero*. It shows three New York City firefighters raising the United States flag onto a flagpole. They stand on the remains of the World Trade Center towers, which became known as "Ground Zero."

How would you describe this photograph? How do you imagine the firefighters were feeling as they raised the flag over such a horrific scene? What message might they have been trying to send? Write a paragraph to answer these questions.